THE ZOO IS CLOSED TODAY!

UNTIL FURTHER NOTICE

By Evelyn Beilenson

ILLUSTRATED BY
Anne Kennedy

Peter Pauper Press, Inc.
White Plains, New York

For Nick, my three children,
John, Larry, and Suzanne, and my
five grandchildren, Sarah, Hannah,
Jacob, Jane, and Tommy

Text copyright © 2014 by Evelyn Beilenson
Illustrations copyright © 2014 by Anne Kennedy
First edition 2014

Published by Peter Pauper Press, Inc.
202 Mamaroneck Avenue
White Plains, New York 10601

Published in the United Kingdom and Europe by Peter Pauper Press, Inc.
c/o White Pebble International
Unit 2, Plot 11 Terminus Rd.
Chichester, West Sussex PO19 8TX, UK

Designed by Heather Zschock

Library of Congress Cataloging-in-Publication Data

Beilenson, Evelyn L.
  The zoo is closed today! / written by Evelyn Beilenson ; illustrated
by Anne Kennedy. -- First edition.
      pages cm
  Summary: Sue and John ask Pete the zookeeper why Kalama Zoo is
closed, and he tells them the animals are ill, from Edward the
elephant who has a cold to Fran the flamingo who has a sore throat.
  ISBN 978-1-4413-1526-7 (hardcover : alk. paper) [1. Stories in
rhyme. 2. Zoo animals--Fiction. 3. Sick--Fiction.] I. Kennedy, Anne,
1955- illustrator. II. Title.
  PZ8.3.B39552Zoo 2014
  [E]--dc23
                        2013040050

ISBN 978-1-4413-1526-7
Manufactured for Peter Pauper Press, Inc.
Printed in Hong Kong

7 6 5 4 3 2 1

Visit us at www.peterpauper.com

THE ZOO IS CLOSED TODAY!

UNTIL FURTHER NOTICE

It was a warm, sunny day
with not much to do.
So Sue and John walked
to the Kalama Zoo.

The gate was shut tight.
All was quiet and still,
since inside the zoo,
the animals were ill.

A sign on the gate
told the kids what to do:
"Be patient and wait,
'til all's well at the zoo."

Then all of a sudden,
from just down the street,
their old friend appeared—
the zookeeper, Pete!

They eagerly asked him
if he could please say
just what was ailing
the animals that day.

He looked worried and weary,
as he shook his gray head.
With a heave and a sigh,
this is what he said . . .

Edward the elephant
has a cold in his nose.
He gets drops up his trunk
through a long garden hose.

The poor bunny's ears
flop down to the ground.
Her earache's no joke—
Beth can't hear a sound.

And Freddy the fox
was having such fun
he forgot his lotion,
and got burnt in the sun.

Marcel the monkey
cannot even swing!
His poor tail is broken
and tied up in a sling.

And Helen the Hippo
has cramps in her tummy.
She ate a bad apple
that she thought would be yummy.

Our black and white zebra
came down with the flu.
Zeke lies in the shade
feeling black, white, AND blue.

Carlos the camel
has red, itchy bumps.
To the doctor's surprise
he has hives on his humps.

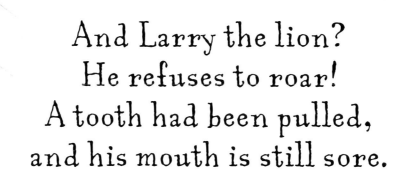

And Larry the lion?
He refuses to roar!
A tooth had been pulled,
and his mouth is still sore.

Poor Fran the flamingo
cannot sing a note.
She gargles and gurgles
to soothe her sore throat.

So now you know
just why they are sick.
But with lots of rest,
they'll get better quick.

Then Pete and the kids said their goodbyes.
They sadly trudged home, with tears in their eyes.

But the very next day
Sue and John got a letter.
The zookeeper said
the animals felt better.

They shouted with glee!
The kids were so pleased.
But first Sue, and then John,
began to sniffle and sneeze.

Now THEY were home sick with nothing to do . . .

...so all of the animals
came to see John and Sue!